Going Places
ON A TRAIN

By Robert M. Hamilton

Gareth Stevens
Publishing

Please visit our website, www.garethstevens.com. For a free color catalog of all our high-quality books, call toll free 1-800-542-2595 or fax 1-877-542-2596.

Library of Congress Cataloging-in-Publication Data

Hamilton, Robert M., 1987-
 On a train / Robert M. Hamilton.
   p. cm. — (Going places)
 Includes index.
 ISBN 978-1-4339-6283-7 (pbk.)
 ISBN 978-1-4339-6284-4 (6-pack)
 ISBN 978-1-4339-6281-3 (library binding)
 1. Railroad trains—Juvenile literature. 2. Railroad travel—Juvenile literature. I. Title.
 TF148.H318 2012
 385—dc23
                              2011031218

First Edition

Published in 2012 by
Gareth Stevens Publishing
111 East 14th Street, Suite 349
New York, NY 10003

Copyright © 2012 Gareth Stevens Publishing

Editor: Katie Kawa
Designer: Andrea Davison-Bartolotta

Photo credits: Cover, pp. 1, 5, 15, 17, 19, 24 (engine) Shutterstock.com; pp. 7, 9, 24 (rails) iStockphoto/Thinkstock; p. 11 Hulton Archive/Getty Images; pp. 13, 24 (steam) FloridaStock/Shutterstock.com; p. 21 Ulrik Tofte/Lifesize/Thinkstock; p. 23 STR/AFP/Getty Images.

All rights reserved. No part of this book may be reproduced in any form without permission in writing from the publisher, except by a reviewer.

Printed in the United States of America

CPSIA compliance information: Batch #CW12GS: For further information contact Gareth Stevens, New York, New York at 1-800-542-2595.

Contents

On the Tracks 4

Parts of a Train 14

Types of Trains 18

Words to Know 24

Index 24

Trains move fast!
They have many wheels.

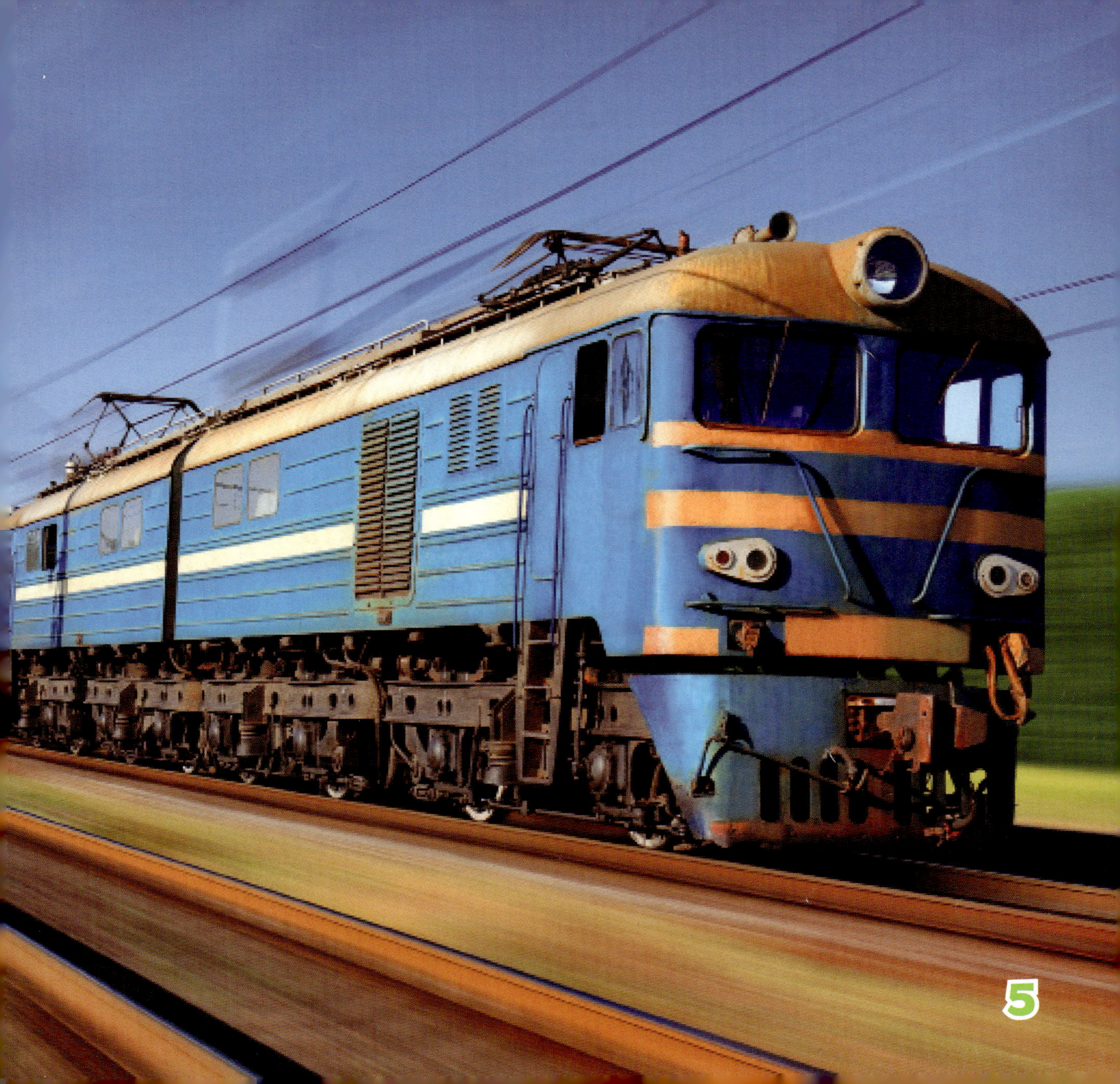

Trains move on tracks.

7

A track is made with two rails.

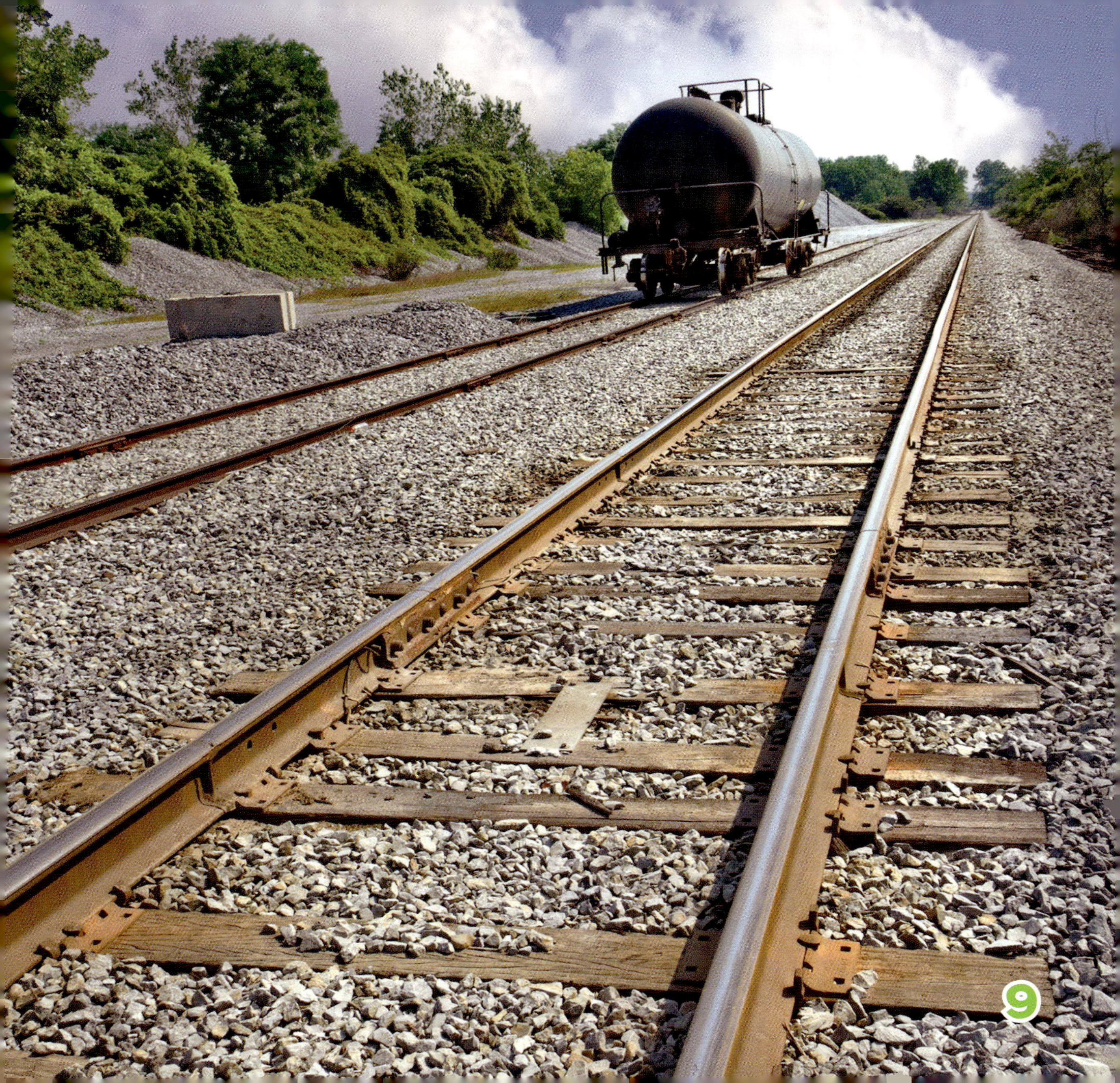

The first trains used horses to move.

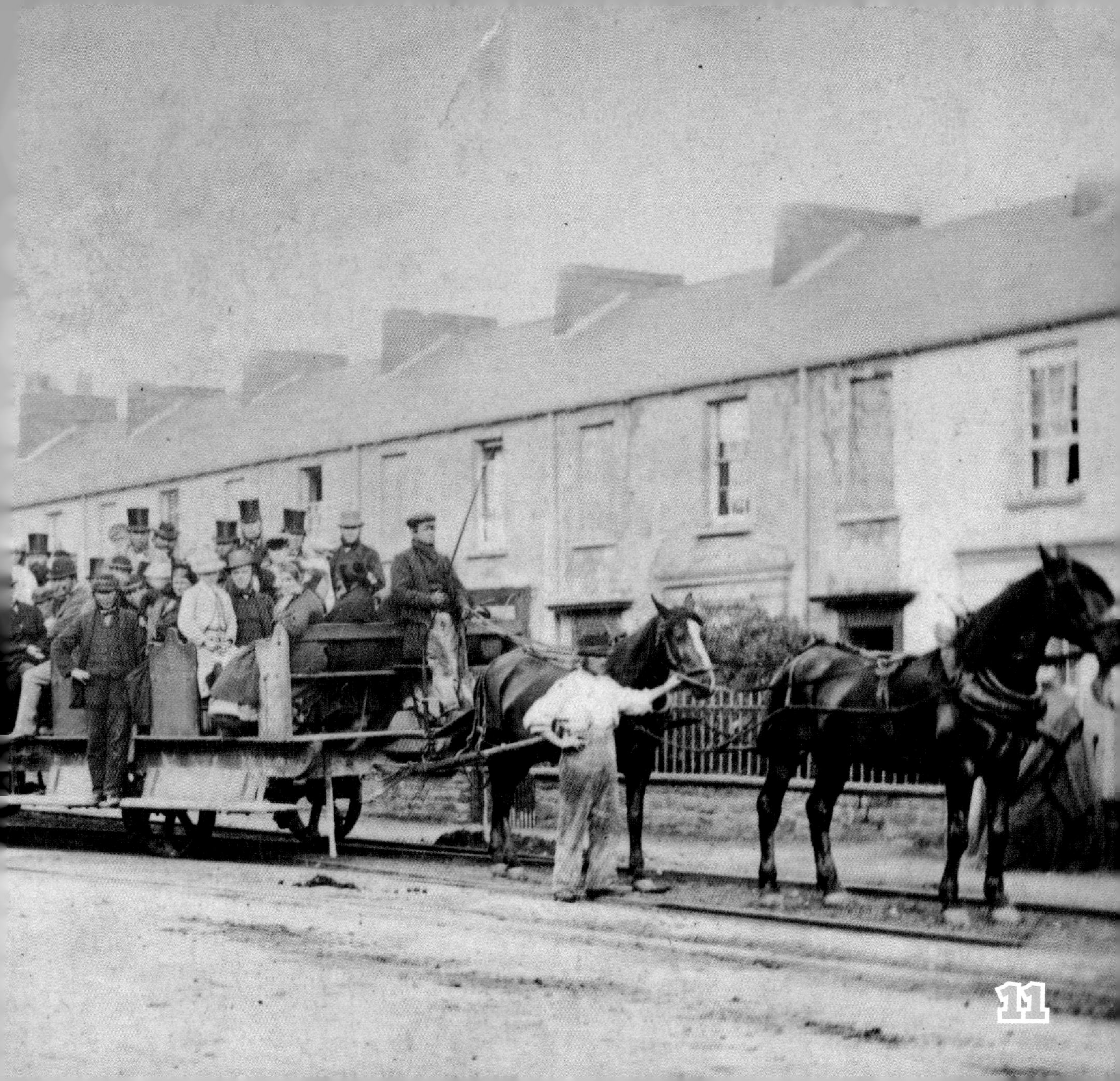

Then, they used steam.

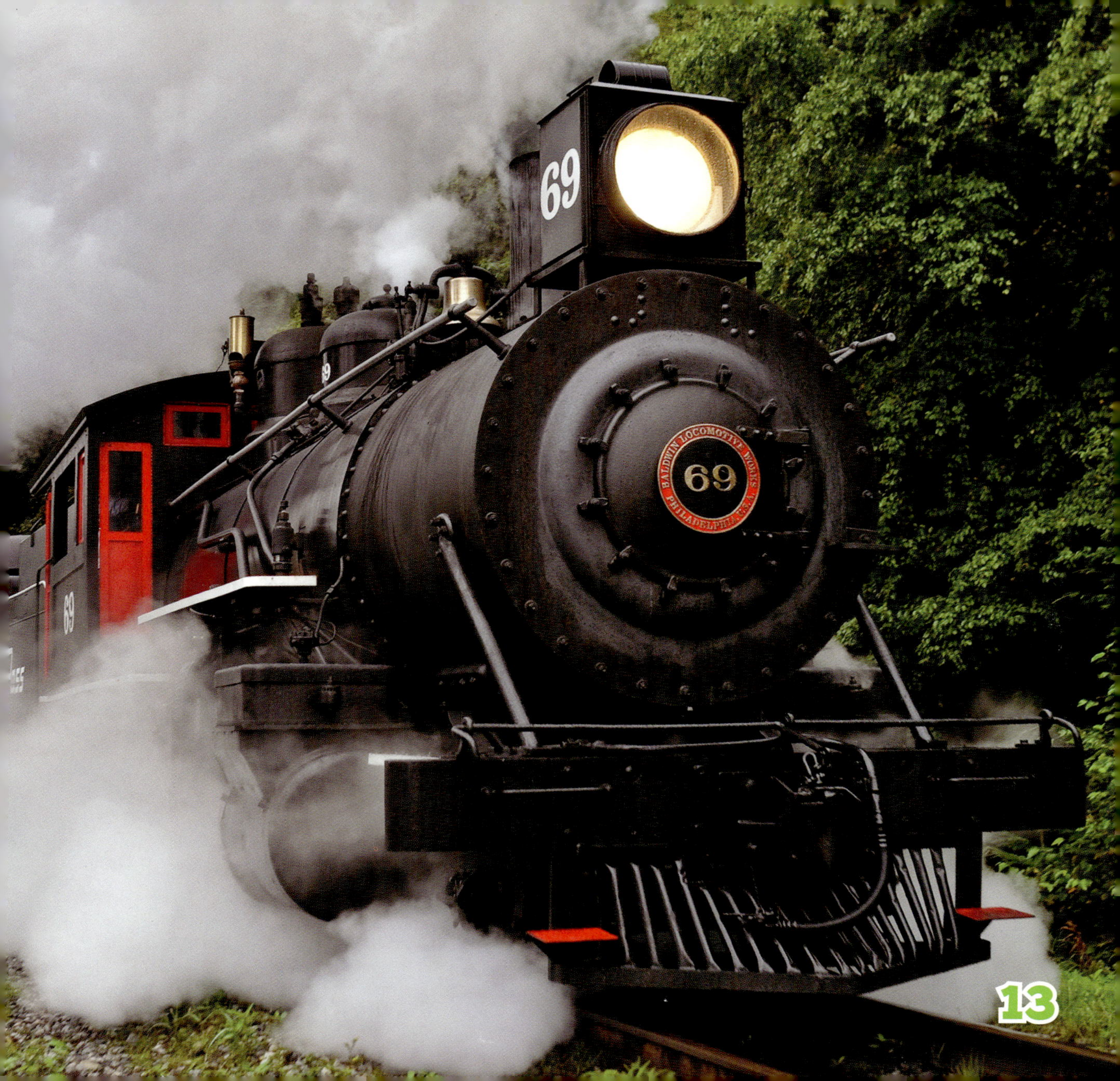
69
BALDWIN LOCOMOTIVE WORKS
69
PHILADELPHIA U.S.A.

The front of the train makes it go.
It is called the engine.

15

Trains have many cars.
The cars hold
things and people.

17

Some trains carry things. These are called freight trains.

19

Some trains carry people. These are called passenger trains.

21

The fastest trains are bullet trains.

23

Words to Know

engine    rails    steam

Index

bullet trains 22   passenger trains 20

freight trains 18   tracks 6, 8